Priya Grewal is from Hounslow, West London, UK. She graduated from University College London with a 2.1 in BA History in 2011. Priya currently lives in Uxbridge, West London and loves reading, watching films and has a passion for writing.

I would like to dedicate this book to my family, whom I wish to thank for supporting me every step of the way with writing.

Priya Grewal

THE CREATOR

AUSTIN MACAULEY PUBLISHERS™

LONDON • CAMBRIDGE • NEW YORK • SHARJAH

A CIP catalogue record for this title is available from the British Library.

ISBN 9781035801923 (Paperback)
ISBN 9781035801930 (ePub e-book)

www.austinmacauley.com

First Published 2023
Austin Macauley Publishers Ltd®
1 Canada Square
Canary Wharf
London
E14 5AA

I would like to thank Austin Macauley Publishers for making my dream come true and publishing *The Creator*. Many thanks.

Chapter 1

Millions and millions of years ago, before anything existed, there was an explosion. In the nothingness, particles began forming and combining and grew more and more powerful until all of a sudden, there was a great explosion. From the explosion came the first life. An entity was born. The entity could think. The entity took the form of a cloud and began wondering...

Who am I? The entity asked itself. The entity could see nothing else in the vast emptiness of nothingness. *Am I the only being in existence?* the entity pondered. Nothing but me...

The entity, a coloured cloud thinking to itself, continued to float around the nothingness and could not believe it was the only thing in existence.

"I know," the entity said to itself. "I will make myself a physical form and will call it a body and carve myself, what I will call, a face."

The entity began envisioning a body. It began forming what it would later call an arm, a leg, a hand, a foot, a torso, a neck and produced a second hand, arm, leg and foot. Next, the entity began envisioning a face. It thought up what it would later call eyes, a nose, and mouth, a tongue, a chin, a forehead and short black hair. The entity made up the colour black for its hair, green for its eyes, formed a straight nose and a chiselled, muscular body. It invented the colour light brown for what it called its skin. Once the entity had fully envisioned its form, body and head, it started to take the form of what it had envisioned. The cloud like form began transforming. When it was fully transformed, it looked at its hands and feet and arms and legs. *If only I could see myself,* thought the entity. The entity produced an object to see itself, in what the entity would later call its mind and conjured up what the entity would call a mirror to look at its full form. The entity admired its own form as an extremely handsome being looked back at itself. Pleased with its appearance, the entity decided to cover itself. It thought up what it would later call a shirt, trousers and shoes and magicked them on itself. It looked in the mirror satisfied with what it would later call clothing. The entity decided to call itself a name, a good name.

"Draconian," the entity mouthed his first word and sound. It decided this would be its name. The entity continued to stare in the mirror and thought about what it had done so far. There was nothing else there. No other beings. Nothing but itself. The entity thought of itself being the first and only being in existence and decided on the word 'god' to call itself and thought of the word male for itself. A male god, a man god. So began the life and existence of Draconian.

Next, Draconian began thinking of a shelter for himself, as he stood in the nothingness with the mirror. He began envisioning a shelter for himself. He began designing something grand in his mind and began inventing in his mind. He thought of long halls and objects and things to sit on and lounge in. When Draconian was done inventing his home in his head, he stretched out his hands and began to produce the grand shelter he had designed for himself and watched what he would call colours leave his hands. When Draconian was finished, he stood proud and looked at his creation. *I will call it a palace,* he thought to himself. *I will call it my home.*

Next, Draconian began designing an incredible land to surround his palace. He designed what he would later call flowers, trees, gardens, forests, waterfalls, lakes and fountains. He designed what he could call an ocean and a sandy beach to accompany it. Once Draconian was done designing, he stretched out hands again and conjured his vision. Once the colours were finished swirling and forming into his vision, Draconian stopped and stared at the beautiful, captivating lands he had made for himself. Draconian took to the air to examine the whole thing. As he flew through the air, he began thinking of something for overhead and stretched out his hands again and transformed the nothingness overheard into what he called a beautiful sky full of what he would call enchanting stars and shooting stars. He thought of there being two skies. One which was bright, that he would call the day and he would make the sky darken into what he would call night. *Time for the shooting stars,* Draconian thought to himself. Draconian admired his beautiful forests, lakes, flowers, trees sand, ocean and sky and eventually flew back to his palace entrance. Draconian looked at his hands and wondered what to call the colours that came from his hands. He decided to call it magic and mouthed his second word out loud. Feeling happy with his lands and sky, he opened what he would call the door to the palace and settled himself into his new home.

Chapter 2

Draconian had settled happily into his palace. He had continued to invent things for his palace and named everything inside and outside the palace. He had designed and conjured indoor and outdoor baths and what he named Jacuzzis in his palace and a swimming pool and had invented an activity called swimming. He enjoyed lounging in his grand garden with a hammock and designed sofas, a bed, chandeliers and eventually began to grow bored after he had named everything. Draconian began to feel lonely in his solo one man-god existence. Then Draconian had a sudden thought.

Why don't I build myself a world? he thought to himself. *Why don't I build myself a world and make beings who look like me and make them palaces and rule over it. I will call myself King,* he thought to himself. *Before I begin creating and designing my population, I will design things for my population to do. I will entertain my population, so they will have a great existence and I will enjoy company and my own inventions too.*

Draconian began designing. He invented what he called food, the most amazing tastes and what he called drinks for exquisite pleasure. He created a language which he called

English, simply by making words out of sounds and naming everything. He created letters and numbers. He invented sports for his population to have fun playing. He invented video games. He began to think of stories and entertaining his population and created what he called films or movies and cartoons. He invented what he called widescreen massive televisions to be in everyone's palaces, what he would put his films on and entertain the population with. He created the cinema for new releases. He made what he called TV shows. He created the theatre. Restaurants. He created beautiful sounds and called it music and made up words with the music and called it a song. He designed and conjured magnificent clubs to play the music in. He invented the radio to listen to songs. He put his stories into word form and created books. He invented moving to the songs and called it dancing. Draconian designed and conjured beautiful parks and hangouts, entertainment complexes. When Draconian thought about the population, he decided to create a new gender. He wouldn't just design males like himself, he would design what he later named a female. He designed a female or woman with what he called breasts, a softer body and longer hair. He made up clothing for both genders. Trousers, skirts, jeans and dresses for women. He designed every being he was going to make a palace to be their home. He planned on making zillions and zillions of males and females. He designed massage parlours, bubble baths, nails, spas and salons for men and women. He made up what he called malls and shops for the population to pick out new clothing and items for themselves and homes, which would magically refill. He made up arcades and theme parks with exhilarating rides. He made beaches and oceans. Make up for women. He decided which magical powers to give to his population. He decided on flying, teleporting, speed, flitting, conjuring and super strength, so they could all enjoy the sports he had invented to go with having superpowers.

He invented the concept of a party and dinners and banquets. He designed boat parties. He invented chocolate, sweets, and many types of meals. He made up breakfast, lunch, dinner and junk food. He invented a calendar, months, days and years. He invented a clock and time so people could arrange get-togethers and called this the date and he too could arrange his own balls, parties and events in his own palace.

When Draconian finished designing and creating his world and all the activities for his population's pleasure and entertainment, he looked ecstatically at the greatest world he could have ever created. He called it his universe. He labelled the different areas countries, cities and planets and gave each planet a name. He created a glorious sky and hangouts in what he called space, where one could see the whole glorious universe. He conjured the palaces for each member of his universe. He had finished designing and creating his incredible universe.

Chapter 3

With his universe complete, all palaces and attractions in place, Draconian made his first being.

"Hello," said Draconian to his first ever creation. He had made a male first, complete with the language he had invented and a range of magical powers. He had made him incredibly handsome with the same skin tone and hair colour as himself, with a chiselled face and nose and muscular body.

"Welcome to my universe. My world, Alaskia (he had named it). I am your maker. Your creator and creator of the universe you will shortly see. Your name is Dreyfus. Come, let me show you your body and face I have sculpted." As Dreyfus got up from the table Draconian had made him upon, he stared amazed at his hands. Draconian led him to the mirror.

"Please, take a look at yourself. I am the first and only being in existence," Draconian explained to him. "I was born from an explosion of elements and sculpted my own face and body and created and made this form, when I was a cloud to begin with." Draconian switched to his original form to show him and then back to his body. "I made myself what I call a home and some lands. Also, I forgot to tell you the name I made for myself. My name is Draconian, the creator of yourself, Dreyfus, and the universe. I was lonely by myself and so decided to make a world, full of beings. You are my first creation and I will make a world with millions and millions of beings. I have equipped you with what I call magical powers to enjoy and have created a world of magical delights for all to enjoy. Now let me show you your palace. Ah, I have named your species, the beings I am making Alaskians. The planet which will be your home Sonoralia, your city, Ronkaria and your town, which will soon be full of neighbours for you to talk to and become friends with, is called Monmaria. I have equipped you so you can use your powers straight away. I'll briefly show you what you can do when I've showed you your palace. I have made you fully ready to communicate. The language I have made is called English. Come, let me show you the universe before showing you your palace."

"Well, thank you, Draconian, for making me. I am honoured to be made first and feel excited to live in and experience the universe you have made," Dreyfus stated, his first ever words.

"I call myself King Draconian," Draconian said. "This is my empire. My universe. I have made the word King for my title as ruler and creator. King and emperor of all beings and my universe, where I wish my creation to have the most wonderful and fantastic of times," King Draconian said as he led Dreyfus to his gardens.

"I call myself a god. The only one with no creator," Draconian stated. Draconian stopped once they had reached his gardens. Dreyfus looked around in amazement at the astonishing garden and sights.

"Now I want you to think the word fly in your head. One of your powers. I will show you my universe," Draconian informed him.

Dreyfus did as advised and felt a thrill of excitement as he began to rise higher and higher into the air and Draconian levelled to meet him.

"Come, let's fly," Draconian laughed.

King Draconian and Dreyfus sailed through the air. Dreyfus felt a rush of exhilaration as he looked at the beautiful, incredible looking lands with exciting attractions and could not believe this was going to be his home. His breath caught in his throat when King Draconian, his creator, showed him what he called space, a view of the entire universe, all the planets and there were even things to do there, in the beautiful cosmos.

"It's incredible, King Draconian," Dreyfus said. "I thank you for making me." King Draconian laughed.

"Next, we will teleport outside the home I have made for you. I call them palaces. Just think my palace in your head and we will be right outside it," said King Draconian.

Dreyfus did as advised and next popped up outside a magnificent building and felt ecstatic about having a palace, as King Draconian had made for himself, as his home. Draconian popped up beside him a split second later.

"Let me show you around and settle you in, but first I will show you everything you can do," King Draconian said. Draconian demonstrated flitting, speed, super strength and conjuring and Dreyfus copied feeling ecstatic.

"Right, let's enter your palace. Your home," King Draconian said. Dreyfus followed amazed as his creator showed him the grandest, most exciting home that could exist.

As well as the grand architecture, there were baths, spas and Jacuzzis for relaxing. Draconian showed him the television for entertainment and music on the radio. He was in awe when he showed him his wardrobe full of clothing and shoes to wear and noted the trousers and shirt he was wearing now. Draconian showed Dreyfus a stunning garden with a swimming pool. Draconian showed him games rooms, an indoor cinema and sports rooms. All sorts of fun things to do. Video games and many other rooms for activities. When it came to showing him food and drink, he nearly squealed in excitement at how good it tasted and could not wait to begin his existence. Draconian also showed him a library full of what he called books, stories he had written and showed him how to switch on the TV.

"Okay," Draconian said. "Welcome again to my world. I will leave you to settle in and begin enjoying your existence. I am going to start making the rest now and introduce them to the universe and their world. You will have company soon. When you have settled into the palace, please feel free to go out and start enjoying yourself at my attractions and take your neighbours with you when they arrive. They'll all be named by myself too. I'll visit after you've had the opportunity to settle in. Goodbye for now," King Draconian said and began to fly away.

"Let me know if you have any questions. You can contact me telepathically just think 'communicate with Draconian'." Dreyfus heard the last words in his head as his creator flew away. Dreyfus turned back around to stare at the palace his creator had made for him.

"Wow," he uttered in sheer amazement.

Chapter 4

Draconian continued to make millions and millions of beings or Alaskians as he called them. Female after male and continued in that order. Each one he named and showed his universe to and showed them how to use their powers and settled them into their palaces. Once the Alaskians had settled in and started befriending one another in their towns in their planets, they went outside to try out the attractions and amusements. Their experience of Draconian's inventions was beyond words, the Alaskians found and cries of joy could be heard from theme parks and happy excited voices could be heard everywhere. The hangouts were full of Alaskians and people could be seen flying happily in space too.

When Draconian was done making and settling zillions and zillions of beings, both male and female into their palaces, he floated invisibly over his universe and took a look at the whole thing. Immensely happy with the zillions he had made and his wonderful empire and pleased with seeing everyone enjoy themselves at the palaces he had made them and at his amusements and attractions, Draconian smiled to himself; ecstatic and proud of his grand empire. The planets, the countries, the cities, the towns, all invented by himself. He travelled back to his own palace and sat on the throne he had fashioned himself. The most powerful being in existence. Emperor Draconian.

Millions and millions of years went by. Emperor Draconian was immensely popular and the people of the universe loved him. They loved his inventions. His empire was a massive industry ran by himself, where he entertained the masses with ongoing music releases, movies, books and plays at his theatres. He delighted the world with his new inventions and attractions for millions of years. His parties were legendary. He was friends with everyone and the universe he had created was actually non-stop fun for eternity. Draconian was described as kind, benevolent, a genius and had the most handsome of faces. His popularity was immense. His genius, adored, admired and celebrated. Draconian himself loved his empire and loved inventing, writing books and inventing everything else he'd made.

***

Meanwhile, in the quiet rooms in the halls of some of the residents across the universe, jealous utterings had been made across the millennias. Small groups of the jealous had formed in the towns in the cities across the universe. They moaned about Draconian, despite his friendship and kindness and magnificent homes he had bestowed upon them all.

"I hate him," remarked Lucian to his friend, Serline, and two males named Feraz and Rozzio. They had been Lucian's secret 'we hate Emperor Draconian' group since the first month of existence and laughed thinking about their equivalents across the universe. Their jealousy was no joke. It consumed them all by now. He hated faking it in front of

Draconian when he invited them around for dinner and lounging. Lucian despised sitting with his creator, wishing for every second he was him, along with his friends. He wished he had the power, the face, the adoration and the popularity. He wished he was called a genius and celebrated the way the universe celebrated Draconian and his inventions. Even as they pleasured in the food, the drink and delights of the world, they despised Draconian. Sometimes they laughed at one another enjoying his inventions and their envy of him. It had started in the first week for Lucian, when Draconian had shown him around his palace and departed. Lucian had gone to look at himself in the mirror again.

"Wow," he said to himself as he admired his form in the mirror. He took off his clothes so he could look at himself fully and turned around and admired his physique. He turned around again and looked at his chiselled face, startling blue eyes, and light brown skin. He admired his chest and torso and muscular arms. He was overcome with his own beauty and body and could not believe how handsomely he had been made.

"What a face," he said to himself, "and what a body."

After that he had said hello to his neighbours and began enjoying the world and attractions, the super arcades and theme park rides and his own gardens and swimming pool, supremely proud of his appearance all the while. He wished he could take a mirror with him everywhere, just so he could look at himself again. Then came Draconian's visit to the town. He gathered all in Lucian's town at one of the halls to officially welcome them all, now he had finished making all the beings for his universe. Lucian attended, supremely happy, still admiring his own form when he noticed something. As he watched his creator, he glanced around as Draconian stood in the centre, the audience seated circularly around him. Lucian noticed that Draconian had the greatest face of all. Lucian looked at the males and females. The females were incredibly beautiful and the men were all handsome with muscular chiselled bodies. Draconian, however, had the most beautiful face of all. The greatest out of all men and women. Lucian looked upon Draconian with envy and thought it had better not be better than his own face. After the welcome and smiling and saying hello to Draconian, Lucian had teleported back to his palace. He stared in the mirror and magically conjured Draconian's face into the mirror and glanced at his own reflection next to it. He wanted to smash the mirror into pieces in fury. Draconian's face was better than his own.

"That's not fair," Lucian had remarked. "He made his face first and it's the best of all. I want his face."

He stared disgruntled, into the mirror, as there was nothing he could do about it and the storm of jealousy grew and grew inside of him, as he watched Draconian at the centre of the stage and as Draconian became a good personal friend to all, including himself. Friendly and humble and powerful. Lucian fake smiled and paid lip service to Draconian, as his jealousy grew and grew hating Draconian's face, and began to envy and loathe everything else too. The centre stage, the admiration for Draconian's creations. The songs, the books, the films, the plays, the fun sports and activities. The architecture. Lucian wished he could gag every time his friends mentioned Draconian. He only approached the three like-minded people as he called them. Serline, Rozzio and Feraz who had lived in the same town, their palaces not far from his, because he had seen them not looking enthusiastic and not respond when a number of them went to dinner and the others were praising Draconian. So Lucian had approached them and commented on not looking enthusiastic like the others and got the sounds and groans he wanted to hear, and made them into his secret gang. The rest he was a fake friend to and wished he could throw something at them every time they mentioned their Creator. The gang all enjoyed themselves and the world all the while, they just envied and loathed Draconian and the admiration and wished his face was theirs. Serline wished hers were more beautiful than his. So they moaned and enjoyed the universe like everyone else for millions of years, eye rolling and gagging wishing they were Draconian. Lucian wanted to be Draconian so badly he said hello to as many he could visit in the city he lived in and visited every planet to try and make friends, just because everyone knew Draconian's name because he made them all and was a friend to all. Lucian wanted that many people to know his name and for them all to admire him. He wanted to be Draconian. He wanted his face, his throne, his power. The admiration. The popularity.

Lucian settled back into his chair, after reflecting on how it had all begun.

"We better go and attend the opening ceremony for the Creator's new attraction," Lucian grumbled. The other three looked moodily back at him.

"His majesty will be expecting us," Lucian remarked sarcastically and the four teleported out.

Chapter 5

Lucian, Feraz and Serline and some others from their town had been invited to dine with their creator at his palace. They laughed and joked and had a grand banquet. After, they went outside to play golf in Draconian's private magical sports stadium.

"Good game," Draconian said to Lucian tapping him on the back.

"How have you been?" Draconian asked Lucian.

"Good, thank you," Lucian replied, jealousy bubbling to the surface as he looked at Draconian, envious to the core of his startling green eyes.

"I really liked your new music releases. I've been lounging in my pool listening to them," Lucian said.

"Oh, thank you," said Draconian. "I thought I'd try out a different kind of sound. Have you tried out the new restaurant in town?" Draconian asked.

"Yes," Lucian said falsely. "I had a wonderful time. When you think you couldn't invent anything better, it gets even better. Even by your own standards," Lucian remarked.

Draconian laughed and said, "Come everyone, back to my palace for drinks."

Lucian followed and caught the eye of Serline briefly. She was caught in a false conversation with one of their friends from the same town, Anrita. Lucian glanced back at the back of Draconian's head wishing he could make him disappear forever.

Chapter 6

Later on that night at 11 pm, Lucian sat on a sofa in his library. He sat in silence, lost in thoughts.

I wish I could make him really disappear, Lucian thought to himself and stared at his hand.

"What if there were a way? Could I conjure magic that could eradicate the entire universe from existence as well as Draconian? Get rid of his fan base too, which would need doing anyway to get away with erasing Draconian from existence, but I'd love to erase them all. Uncreate all of them. Destroy the love for Draconian and the popularity. The whole universe eradicated," Lucian mused to himself.

First of all, I'll see how many are jealous of Draconian throughout the entire universe and see if a plan can be made, Lucian thought to himself.

"Show me those who despise Draconian, across his universe," Lucian said, hand outstretched and an image formed in front of him showing how many there were. In the population of zillions and zillions, there were many.

"What figure is that?" asked Lucian.

One third of the entire population, the words appeared before him.

So, Lucian thought to himself, *two thirds of the population love the Creator and one third envy and loathe him. It's enough,* he stated.

How can I eradicate the two thirds along with Draconian from existence? Lucian thought.

"What if I could conjure a magical energy so hot it could eradicate our very form? Melt them into nothing," Lucian muttered to himself.

Lucian conjured a chair in front of himself and started conjuring an orange energy ball in his hand. "Make it as hot as it can get. Conjure to eradicate," Lucian commanded.

Lucian threw the orange energy ball at the chair and it was reduced to cinders. A black mark was all that was left on the floor, where the chair had been. A black stain on his floor.

"Yes!" Lucian said out loud. *I will use it on Draconian and the entire universe,* he thought. "Wait," he said to himself.

"Will this work on Draconian and the entire universe?" Lucian asked himself.

"Show me what happens if I throw it at Draconian," he commanded.

An image swirled in front of him. The orange energy ball flew towards Draconian. He briefly glowed orange and nothing else happened.

"Curse them all," Lucian muttered furiously.

"Show me what happens if I use it on everyone in the universe" Lucian commanded.

A new image swirled in front of him. The image showed him the entire universe being reduced to nothing in his orange magic; a flame with it and screaming.

"Yes," Lucian said victoriously. *Now what to do with Draconian?* Lucian thought for a few moments.

What about a prison dimension? he thought. "Can I transport him to a prison dimension, where it is impossible for him to use his powers? Show me," he commanded. This time the image showed Lucian throwing another energy ball, which hit Draconian and transported him into a prison dimension and he cried out in fury as he could not use his powers in the prison dimension, after the initial confusion, about where he was.

"Got you," said Lucian silkily to himself. "I think I'll make it the most hellish dimension I can, your imperial majesty," Lucian added, as he looked with loathing at Draconian's eyes, "for all of eternity."

"Destruction for Draconian's universe and my friends who love him," Lucian stated, "and a hell prison dimension for Draconian…forever," Lucian shrieked victoriously.

"Now all I have to do is recruit Serline, Feraz and Rozzio and persuade them into doing it and persuade them to help me persuade one third of the population into killing everyone in the universe, while the four of us transport Draconian into his torture prison. We can multiply, so we can destroy all in the universe and send our duplicates to everyone on the universe whilst myself, Feraz, Serline and Rozzio transport Draconian into his prison dimension. We can turn invisible and float so there is nothing for us to fear. No sound and the rest can do the same. I will make a replica hideaway in case we fail with a security alarm so if there any magical breach attempts on it, the alarm will sound and we will teleport into the next hideaway. If there's an attempt on the next one, the alarm sounds again and we'll be gone again into the next one. Draconian will never be able to capture us. I just need to replicate this universe as our hide away. Same homes," Lucian laughed.

"Who will say no if they're as jealous as I am," Lucian stated. "What can go wrong if we're invisible and floating? No sound," Lucian remarked.

"I'll be idolized," Lucian said. "A hero to all who envy and despise Draconian. I'll get the glory. I'll be the king. The emperor; of destruction, of Draconian's Hell prison. The key master. One third of the universe will bow before me. Not only will I get rid of Draconian and destroy all in his universe who love him. I'll have the glory. The admiration. Everyone will bow before me. I will rule the universe. I'll be the emperor. The emperor of chaos and destruction. Master of the universe. The universe will be mine. I don't need a title. I don't need a crown. I'll have the glory. The worship. I'll be the new Draconian. What's not to love? Draconian imprisoned in Hell, his fans gone. The universe will be ours. It will be mine. Time for the jealous to reign," Lucian said to himself.

"It's a great plan," Lucian said to himself. "Right, time to get started," he said.

"I'll visit Serline first." Lucian teleported out of the room.

Chapter 7

"An entire world universe takeover?" Serline asked, curious and perplexed as Lucian sat in her palace living room with Feraz and Rozzio.

"Yes," said Lucian. "What can go wrong if we're floating (no sound) and invisible? Then we'll be the monarchs. The Emperor. The Kings. All of us. Us four will be celebrated forever for planning and organising it, if you help me persuade one third of the universe's population. They just need to duplicate; the duplicates will mimic the action of the third throwing my destruction magic at every member of the population all located by the duplicates, and everyone on every planet will be destroyed in the same moments. Everyone can be assigned to their own planet. The Draconian despisers are all across the universe, few lone ones with no one to express their hatred to," Lucian said.

"Imagine it," Lucian said, "us four, the replacement of Draconian. The admiration. The glory. One third of the population knowing our names, worshipping us. Celebrating us forever. No titles. No emperor. No king. No creator. Of course we still enjoy the palaces and inventions of his forever. Thanks, Draconian," Lucian laughed.

"The rest of them obliterated, gone forever and Draconian tortured in a prison hell dimension forever, power bound, as my destruction magic doesn't work on him. We simply need to transport him there magically," Lucian sated.

"I like it," Feraz said.

"I like it a lot," Rozzio said

"And you?" Lucian asked Serline. "Do you love it?"

"I do," said Serline. "I'm just a little nervous about transporting Draconian," she murmured.

"What's to be nervous about? We'll be invisible. We could teleport in now invisibly and transport him into it. We just need to recruit the one third so they destroy the universe population, so we can get away with it. Lucian's designed an impenetrable hideaway with an alarm where we teleport out as soon as there is any breach attempt on it and we'll be gone in a split second. The hideaway is a replica of here. Same homes. We can never be caught and the hideaway is just in case we fail. With invisibility, floating, it's a sure thing. Practically 100 per cent chance of success. What could go wrong? One energy ball of destruction from the rest duplicated, the entire universe wiped out. Transportation and torture for Draconian," Feraz stated.

"We'll be celebrated forever, Draconian reduced to nothing but our powerless toy in our prison and his fans eradicated. Gone forever. We'll be worshipped. No one over us and we'll convince the one third with calling it the free world. No Draconian. Our world and universe only," said Rozzio.

"Us four on top!" Lucian added. "The saviours."

"Okay," said Serline excitedly. "I'm in."

"So," Lucian said. "You three are going to visit the one third with me. I'll add their name to a contract once they've said yes. Once they're recruited and practically bow to us."

"How do you know they'll bow to us?" asked Serline.

"Such is the nature of jealousy," said Lucian. "It's what I'd do, practically bow to anyone who had a way of destroying Draconian and his fan base. Especially when we loathe and envy his face and want his green eyes. Practically wish I could skin him and put it on myself," Lucian added.

"Torture for eternity will do," laughed Serline.

"Who to visit first?" asked Rozzio laughing.

Chapter 8

Lucian, Feraz, Rozzio and Serline had got half the signatures required for the massacre take over and imprisoning and torture of Draconian. They laughed happily in their quarters as the worship began. The billions who had already signed were practically lifting them on their shoulders.

"Down with Draconian!" Many of them celebrated in their palaces, in the shadow of their worlds.

"And his fans too!" they added.

"So sick of them praising him all the time," some said.

Some celebrated wiping out the entire universe and torturing Draconian for eternity. They said yes over their own vanity at the beginning of existence, for their own forms, and were consumed with the same envy of Draconian's face and had not moved on to being jealous of himself as a monarch. They envied his face and didn't like hearing praise for him due to their envy. Now their day had come. An opportunity to destroy him. Many just found destroying their own friends and the universe population a necessity. Only because they had to, to overthrow and torture Draconian forever, the object of their envy.

"Sorry, guys!" many said comically.

"Who's the king now?" one shouted.

Many were excited to use the destruction magic invented by Lucian on their friends and the entire universe.

It turned into the secret world, unbeknown to Draconian and the friends of all who said yes and the four's own circle of friends and best friends. Sitting with them. Laughing with them. Planning on wiping every single one of them from existence. False smiles to Draconian himself. Trying not to sound too overboard whilst talking to him to avoid suspicion. No behaviour different to usual, advised Lucian so there is no suspicion. No extra sucking up, he advised. Don't go overboard and arouse any suspicion, he instructed. Lucian enjoyed the hero worship most of all. Feraz, Serline and Rozzio enjoyed their share too. Serline got annoyed once with Lucian, with it being his plan and invention getting the most praise of all but loved her own glory too much to care about her second of envy.

This or nothing, she thought. *If it weren't for Lucian, there would be nothing at all. We'd still be four, like the rest loathing Draconian behind closed doors and faking it with the rest and I do love getting rid of Draconian and his universe. Equal to enjoying the glory,* she thought to herself.

How the mighty have fallen, she thought to herself, looking at an image of Draconian's prison hell dimension of torture as they called it. "Or will fall," she said out loud.

All four loved the one third knowing their names.

"It's better than I thought it'd be," said Feraz.

"The Four Kings. Emperors of Destruction," said Rozzio.

"Torturers of Draconian," said Feraz. Lucian laughed.

"You never truly live until the whole universe knows your name and worships you," Lucian stated. "And we're destroying the rest!" he laughed.

Lucian conjured up the contract with the billions of names on it so far. He had approached all with the other three. They began their proposal quietly, slowly. Not erratically. Calm and controlled. He took the other three to make the ones they were asking more confident by seeing all four of them in on it. Lines bouncing back and forth with the three after outlining his proposal to each person, helped persuade them all. The other three already being in on it swayed any of the uncertain or nervous, despite them all wanting it. Some shouted and celebrated in excitement as soon as they signed. Some were jovial as soon as he told them his idea. Many signed with glee. Some enjoyed the idea of torturing Draconian, more than wiping him from existence like the others.

"Even better," some said when Lucian told them his destruction magic didn't work on Draconian, so it would be torture instead.

The secret world of faking it in front of the non-suspicious and celebrating in the shadows continued. Others going to visit those who had signed up across the universe, whispering. The eradicators some of them called themselves. The Destroyers, others named themselves. Others called themselves masters of destruction and praised Lucian for his conjuring and hell dimension of torture for Draconian. Genius, others said and celebrated the four visiting them all. Each assigned to destroy their own planet and duplicate to destroy every citizen. Those they did know. Those they didn't. Some had been best friends with those they planned to wipe out for millions of years and of course were friends with their creator too. The secret world continued, the shadow ever growing, until Lucian and the three had the signature of every individual in the jealous one third of the population, located by Lucian, all persuaded by the four into signing his contract of destruction. Destruction and torture they had signed up for. A universe takeover via both. Recruitment was complete.

Chapter 9

It was the evening before, the evening before the massacre of two thirds of the entire universe and imprisoning Draconian in a power bound torture prison hell dimension for eternity. Lucian had visited all with Serline, Feraz and Rozzio to ensure everyone knew what to do and had watched them all practise teleporting, turning invisible, duplicating and throwing his incineration magic to reduce all to nothing. He had ensured they were duplicated so every individual in the universe had a duplicate to incinerate themselves. The plan was slick and everybody was ready to incinerate the following day at 12 pm midday. Himself, Serline, Feraz and Rozzio were to teleport to wherever Draconian was and transport him to his torture prison for eternity. The majority of the rest assigned to incinerating their own planet.

Almost time, Lucian thought to himself in his own chambers, sitting on the chair where he had first began formulating the plan.

I did it, thought Lucian.

I recruited one third of the universe into destroying two thirds of the population and torturing Draconian forever. Glory is almost mine, he thought. "The hour is almost upon us." Nervousness and excitement consumed him. Excited anticipation. He couldn't wait to transport Draconian into a torture dimension and eradicate his population into nothingness. "Once it is done," Lucian said to himself, "the name Lucian will be celebrated forever."

Chapter 10

It was 12 pm the following afternoon. Two thirds of the population were relaxing in their palaces, lounging with their friends, eating at restaurants, or enjoying themselves in one of Draconian's attractions or amusements in the cities they had inhabited, and had the most wonderful of times in for millions of years. Whilst they relaxed and talked and enjoyed themselves, unbeknown to them, what many of their own friends, best friends for some were planning, figures began teleporting into different palaces across the universe. Large groups of them across the cosmos. Invisible. Not one could see them hovering in the air around them. Moments later, screams filled the air across the universe, as the entire population was a flame with Lucian's orange destruction magic. They screamed as the lethal magic was so hot, they felt excruciating searing pain for the first time in their long, joyous existence. Where moments before there had been a happy population enjoying themselves, seconds later there was nothing. It only took seconds to be incinerated into nothing. The universe was silent. Empty. Every town, city, country and planet completely emptied. Population destroyed, massacred. The one third stood victorious.

In the exact same moments, Lucian, Serline, Feraz and Rozzio teleported invisibly to wherever Draconian was. He was sitting in his own chambers watching his own television. He glanced and saw an object move on his mantle. He gasped and fear rose in his throat at the sinister scene he had never witnessed before. He abruptly put a shield up so no magic could touch him.

"Show yourself," he commanded and to his shock saw the faces of those he had made millions of years ago. Lucian, Serline, Feraz and Rozzio. All from a town he named Ferlonia, a planet he'd named Kerazlia. He watched as energy balls hit his shield of protection. He saw the look of fury on Lucian's face and eagerness met with quick panic from the other three. They teleported out before he could say another word or move an inch. With fury and confusion, Draconian teleported from his own palace to the nearest planet and saw it was completely empty. He teleported to the next one, with his shield up and to the next. Everywhere was empty. Only eerie disturbing silence filled the air.

"Show me what happened," he commanded. He saw the face of Lucian, followed by Serline, Feraz and Rozzio and saw and listened to them recruiting the others and showing them all orange magic. Then he watched them turn invisible duplicate and throw the orange magic at every individual and friend he had made and watched as they were incinerated into nothing.

"Noooooo," he cried to himself. He magically put security up around the entire universe so none of the perpetrators could get back inside and checked to make sure no one was still there invisibly. He had listened to the plan for himself. The lethal magic of Lucian's didn't work on himself as they planned to transport himself into a torture prison dimension where they would torture him for eternity. A power bound prison, where he'd be unable to use his powers. Draconian felt betrayed by those he had made and befriended. He made them the greatest palaces he could make, gave them powers, a universe to enjoy forever and they had conspired against him, destroyed their own friends and tried to put him in a torture prison. Themselves torturing him forever. Draconian put up magic so it was not possible for anything alternate to incinerating to occur, so he was completely safe. Next, he outstretched his hands and said,

"Bring them all back." *Please let this work,* he thought. There was a bright light that travelled and filled the air and sky. Moments later, everyone who had been incinerated stood or sat where they had been with confusion and dismay on their face.

What was that excruciating feeling? the population thought as they looked at one another in dismay.

One moment we're sitting, the next an unbearable feeling and then nothing.

Their first thoughts were to themselves. Then they heard Draconian's voice amplified for all to hear,

"I am extremely sorry," said Draconian. "We have been betrayed. One called Lucian from Ferlonia on the planet Kerazlia with three friends, organised destroying the entire universe. He invented magic to eradicate you all from existence. He knew it wouldn't work on me, magically checking himself. His three friends called Serline, Feraz and Rozzio teleported invisibly into my palace. I saw an object move and put a shield up. I turned them visible and saw them throwing energy balls. They teleported out before I could contain them. They were trying to transport me to a torture prison for eternity, power bound, their prisoner and torture victim. The others have also fled. They were invisible around you all when they did it and duplicated to destroy every citizen. I have put security up so they can't get back in. None are in the universe hiding invisibly, I have checked. The universe is completely safe. They can't get back in and I have put magic up so no alternate plans can be done in the future. I cannot be eradicated from existence. I will pass this power on to every single one of you, so this can never happen again."

Moments later, every single citizen was a glow with blue magic for a few seconds. Draconian said, "No magic can ever harm any citizen ever again. No one can be destroyed. You will exist forever as you were all made to do. No alternate plans can take place either. Alaskia is completely safe. Please resume what you were doing and carry on having a good time. I will visit each every single one of you when I can. I will amplify my voice with further information and update the television with everything I can. I will put the scene on television for you all to watch also. I will get back to you as soon as I know where they are. I just want to assure you Alaskia is completely safe." Draconian's voice disappeared as he retreated back to his palace to find out where his enemies had gone. The population of Alaskia slowly returned to what they were doing or went to their palaces in groups to watch the occurrence and events leading up to on television.

Chapter 11

"NOOOOOOO," Lucian screamed as he fell to his knees in defeat. Serline, Feraz and Rozzio beside him on the ground, looking defeated. The four had planned to secretly flee to their own hideaway away from the rest in case they turned on themselves, in case of failure.

"We were so close," Lucian stated.

The four had teleported out of Draconian's palace as soon as their transportation energy balls hit him, and they heard him say "show yourself" at the same time, with his shield up. They teleported out straight away. Draconian's face shocked at the sight of them and telepathically communicated to the one third to flee. *Flee to the hideaway, we failed.* They heard one communicate back, "we succeeded," before disappearing forever.

"It was my fault," said Feraz. "My elbow hit an object on his mantle when I teleported in. He must have seen it move," he groaned.

Cursed Feraz, thought Lucian.

"We didn't plan well enough," said Serline. "Lucian thought of turning invisible and floating for no sound, but we didn't think of bumping into anything when we teleported in."

"Who would have thought of it in palaces so large?" said Rozzio.

"There is no point turning on each other," Rozzio added, "It was Lucian's plan anyway, and now the four of us are in a replica of Draconian's universe, same palaces, forever."

"We agreed to the possibility of failing and living as a four. We're fake with our former friends anyway and the one third are strangers from across the cosmos. They'd turn on us in a second and kill us and they were just acquaintances in the one third from our own country," Rozzio said.

"We'll be bored if we kill any one of us," he added.

Lucian said, "You're right. We all said yes to this outcome."

"We're never going to be kings or a female one now," Serline said.

"Looks like we've got our own land," she added. "No Draconian."

"Do you think we need to be scared of him?" she asked.

"No," said Lucian. "He can never get to us. It's impossible with the alarm. We're gone again as soon as he tries to touch the hideaway with magic. It's a futile chase. May as well laugh at him for bothering," said Lucian.

The four looked at each other. Failed. They had failed to transport Draconian into their hell prison for torture and the rest succeeded in killing the rest of the universe.

"He'll probably bring them all back," said Feraz.

"May as well not have bothered," he added.

"Well, we don't have to put up with his fan base," said Serline. "Draconian's face endures forever," she added. "Not to be our puppet to fling around for eternity."

The four had nothing to do but look at one another. The only beings the four would see for all of eternity.

All my glory gone, thought Lucian. *I was just so close to using everyone to replace him.*

Eerie, disappointed silence filled the air.

***

Meanwhile, in the other hideaway, the one-third roared.

"Where are they?" one called Kaliran roared.

"Is anyone getting anything by telepathically communicating with them," a female named Aliana said.

"Nothing," one named Bazilo responded, looking angry and dangerous.

"Are they anywhere?" shouted Kaliran in their mimic hideaway, the huge colossal number of them grouped together, many floating in the air still.

"It looks like they've fled to their own hideaway," a female called Ashlana said. "All four of them, rather than us turn on them and incinerate them too."

"Curse them," Kaliran screamed. "Not even here to face us."

"How could they fail?" he shouted. "All they had to do was turn invisible and throw an energy ball. We all succeeded. What was the difference?" he roared.

"They tried to imprison a god," said Bazilo. "We destroyed the same species as ourselves. I got so excited when the last message in was Draconian's in his palace. Let's go and teleported to incinerate all."

"We were the fools who thought we could imprison a god. He who made us and gave us our powers. We were fools to go up against him," Aliana stated.

"They were clumsy oafs," Kaliran shouted.

"At least there's many of us, instead of four together like themselves," said Aliana.

"Also, Draconian can never get to us with the alarm system," she added.

"I thought we'd succeed. It seemed so easy turning invisible," Kaliran snapped.

"Looks like the majority thought so too," Bazilo added, observing the furious faces.

He amplified his voice for all to hear.

"They've fled," he said. "Lucian, Serline, Feraz and Rozzio. Into their own hideaway. No one can reach them."

The one third groaned and shouted.

"We must embrace what we agreed to. Life in the replica hideaway. Same homes. They failed to transport Draconian to his hell prison for torture and Draconian's probably brought back everyone we incinerated. We live here together for eternity without the four. Peacefully and harmoniously. There is no way Draconian can get to us with the alarm. It will be a futile chase. We'll have to resume living with Draconian's inventions. There's nothing else we can do."

Bazilo switched his voice back to normal as many began teleporting and flying away to bars and hang outs and their palaces with one another. To groan and groan.

"I felt so powerful and victorious when I incinerated my own friend," said Ashlana. "I wanted to dance and shout with joy. I was so confident. I can't believe the four fled into their own one."

"We would have incinerated them after a few seconds," Bazilo said. "They're watching their own backs."

"Well, isn't that clever," said Kaliran, seething.

"Not clever enough," said Aliana. "We failed."

"We succeeded," Kaliran shouted, "they failed."

"I guess it's our own universe now, in the hideaway, with nothing to fear from Draconian, forever more," said Ashlana.

They stood silently, the rest teleporting into their own palaces and amusements in the replica of Draconian's universe.

"Nothing else can be done," Ashlana added.

Kaliran roared again and teleported out in his fury.

The other three looked at one another disappointedly, feeling deflated and contemplated eternity in their hideaway together.

Chapter 12

"He's gone," Rozzio told Feraz and Serline.

"What do you mean he's gone?" asked Serline.

A few moments earlier, Lucian had said he was just going to pop into his replica palace for a second and would be back in a moment. He had teleported out before anyone could say anything. Rozzio had teleported out a couple of minutes later.

"I got suspicious about his abrupt teleportation so went to see what he was up to," said Rozzio.

"I saw it was empty and called out to him, and communicated telepathically. No response. I enquired magically about his location and saw him on his own, in his own hideaway. We're never going to see him again. We've been telepathically cut off like we did to the others. He must have got paranoid about us turning on him and incinerating him," said Rozzio.

"Curse him to the torture chamber he made for Draconian," said Feraz. "I can't believe he ditched us, on top of everything else."

"We would have turned on him eventually," said Serline. "You both know it and I know it."

"Well, I'm not going anywhere. I want company," said Feraz.

"Don't incinerate me. You'll just get bored without me anyway, with just the two of you. Three is better than two even with Draconian's inventions to enjoy. I guess he thought he'd be okay alone with his grand palace and Draconian's empty universe of creations," Feraz added.

"We won't kill you," said Serline, "it was his grand plan. He missed a step and excited us and we didn't think about anything moving when we teleported in."

"Maybe I'll keep a shield up just in case, like Draconian put up. Our downfall," said Feraz. "Going to be a great eternity with you," said Serline.

"Just the three of us for eternity," said Rozzio.

"Lucian the cursed fled. Us fled from the third. Living in hideaways, hiding from our creator for eternity. Three of them. Three hideaways. At least we're still living in luxury," said Rozzio.

"Hiding in luxury," Serline said.

"At least we have TV. There are still loads of films of Draconian's I haven't seen yet," she added.

"Don't remind me," said Rozzio.

"We're traitors enjoying our maker's inventions and homes he made us," he said.

"We were so close to glory and being him," Rozzio said deflated again.

"To exist in three hideaways for eternity" said Serline.

"That's right," said Feraz, "and you'll never beat our alarms, Draconian."

"Bye, Draconian," said Serline.

"Sorry we massacred everyone else," said Feraz.

Rozzio managed to laugh.

"We just didn't get our maker into a torture chamber for eternity," he added.

"I'm going to drown my sorrows in my Jacuzzi," said Serline and teleported out.

Feraz looked at Rozzio.

"Let's go eat," he said.

Chapter 13

Lucian sat in his own Jacuzzi with his favourite drink. Fled as he planned to. He'd secretly planned to go to his own one, only if it looked like the others were going to turn on him, preferring to have company than no company but willing to flee if he had to. Rozzio had pointed out it was his plan 'anyway' around three seconds in, so he had fled and pretended he was going to his palace for a moment.

He stared into space glowering at his failure. Feeling disappointed and furious. All he could do was enjoy Draconian's luxury home for himself and his empty universe. He still had the TV, movies, shows and music.

May as well put the television, on he thought to himself and magically switched the one in his Jacuzzi room on.

"King and emperor of my own palace now," he muttered to himself, "and this empty replica universe. At least our creator can never get passed my alarm," he said to himself.

"I'm hiding in luxury. So close to replacing and torturing him forever. Destroying the others successful," he said to himself. "I just didn't think of anything moving. Cursed Feraz," he said to himself. "But they blame me," he muttered. "Oh well. You'll never see me again," said Lucian.

"I'm living on my own," he added, "for eternity.

He continued to stare blankly at the television screen.

Chapter 14

Some time had passed in Alaskia. Draconian helped his universe come to terms with the failed atrocity and betrayal for those who had been friends or best friends with the culprits. He himself, who was good friends with all he had created, felt shocked and betrayed, especially after the grand homes he had made them and incredible universe of inventions and entertainment and amusements he had created. He had put the list and pictures of culprits on one of his television channels and showed the history leading up to the atrocity. He had invented the words murder and killed and death or dead for being eradicated and the action, instead of saying destroyed all the time. He could not believe Lucian, the most complimentary of all about his inventions, was the organiser. He supposed now, it was a result of being two faced after viewing the groups or factions, as he thought of it, uttering their words of jealousy for millions of years. He couldn't believe the recruited one third of traitors said yes after their millions of years of bitching, as he called it, because they'd loved their form and faces, that he had made them so much at the beginning of their existence and their own reflections in the mirror, that they could not stand his face being the best of all and everyone else's astonishing beauty level being the same. It was not his fault his face was unbeatable. They would not even exist or have the form he created if he had not created it. There was nothing he could do about making his own face first and no others being better than it. He could not believe they all said yes to annihilate the entire universe, their own friends and best friends, just so they could torture him in Lucian's designed torture prison they called Hell and squat in his universe celebrating. Hence, how Lucian would be his replacement; him and Serline, Rozzio and Feraz glorified, too. He had created the word evil to describe them. The monsters. It was what they were. Murderers. Only Lucian had moved on to being jealous of his creation powers and being ruler of his universe and was jealous of everyone in the universe knowing Draconian's name, as he had made them all and was good friends to all and socialised with all, and threw his own parties in his own palace with every town. Lucian moaned about being a nobody to the other three, and the four tried to acquaint themselves with the entire city they lived in, turning into strange, weird wannabes of himself. Lucian moaned about the glory and praise for his universe and creations from the others for millions of years. So Serline, Feraz and Rozzio had succumbed to his bribe of shared glory if they helped him persuade one third of the universe, the jealous located, into killing the entire universe population whilst they transported him into Lucian's designed Hell for himself. The resurrected thanked the universe for Draconian and the three failing with him, due to Draconian noticing the object on his mantle move and putting his shield up so he could resurrect them all, when they all loved their glorious, pleasure filled existence. They wanted to be the replacement kings and emperors; Serline, empress, of destruction and evil with Lucian's lethal killing magic conjuring. It could never be used again, now he had transferred over the power to not be killed by one another, to his good creations and friends and nothing alternate could be done either. His universe was completely safe, no harm or evil possible. The evil ones could not get back in, even if they could, it would be a wasted trip, all there would be to do was leave again. His only problem was all of them in their hideaways. Three of them. One third appearance envy only, in one. The four had fled to their own one as planned, in secret from the third, in case of failure and he thought of their hideaway as appearance jealousy originally turned into power ambitions through Lucian. Last of all, being paranoid about the three of them killing himself due to failure, Lucian had abandoned the three and was hiding in his own hideaway. Draconian had looked at their magical security designed by Lucian. He could not breach the hideaways with his own powers because as soon as his magic tried to breach the hideaway, an alarm would sound and they'd all be into the next one. It would be a useless, futile chase, so he did not bother attempting for them all to teleport into the next one and cackle at him. The hideaway was well designed by Lucian. An impossible thing, to transport them to himself. He knew the punishment for themselves would be execution as he called it. Lucian's own weapon used by them all on Draconian's population done back to themselves. This was also for attempting to transport their creator into a torture dimension for eternity. He could not think of a way to transport evil, strip them of their powers, sentence and execute them all. He used the word enemies for them. Villains. Mass murderers. Evil. He did not know how to transport them all to himself, as Lucian had planned. Draconian's entire universe named the murderers their enemies. Their failed murderers, thanks to Draconian. Fortunately, his universe was so great, his friends and population still managed to enjoy themselves moments later, the friends and best friends of them all dealing with their betrayal and how they had all socialised with them once they said yes, knowing they were going to kill them all, along the with the whole universe. Draconian too named them demons, for the time they said yes and sat with himself and people of his universe. Villains. Scum, for all he'd created for them. The anger and rage from all, despite enjoying themselves after the failed massacre was understandable. All despised the failed murderers and hated them. Draconian had no way to get to them and was at a loss about what to do about his enemies, the villains in their hideaways.

Chapter 15

Draconian was in his palace working on a new body and sculpting a face. He had come up with a plan. He had been thinking about the torture power bound prison Lucian had designed for himself and had been struck with an idea. He had thought about connecting, breaching and transportation magic to emotions and wondered with enough pressure in a torture situation, if the emotions could speed up the transportation magic and make it breach the hideaway and transport the failed killers before the alarm could go off. He had used his magic to see what would happen in a torment situation and it had worked. He then wondered how he could put a being made by himself in a torment situation and get the constant speed to transport the zillions and zillions of killers and the four. How would he be able to place a being in his idea, a fake world situation of robots without knowing it? Then the idea came to him. He would make an infant version of himself and his population, without powers and no idea about magic being real and would let it grow from what he'd call a baby to full grown. It would grow and develop and learn to talk as it was trained mentally without knowing it, in what he would call school and university and would have no idea that is was growing up being trained by his robots, and he would make up lessons for it and de-threaten the situation so it was not scared at full grown 23 when he changed what the being thought was the planet into a warp, through the appearances of the robots. The torment and torture he would use, he would call gang stalking. He would set up privacy issues and place the existence of magic in his books. He would make the being paranoid and worried about being followed with fears put into the fake world, like killing. The being would be safe from the real universe, as the others could not get in and would have the power not to be killed and would stop aging at 23 and not see the magical transportation vortex leaving it. He would set up a recovery learning bridge plan for once it was over, to safely transition the individual, his transporter, to the real universe. He would put his own identity in as God and put in something called religions, different theories on him and make up a different theory of existence and call it science and introduce prayer into it, so the being had faith. He would make up stories in the religions and call them messengers. He would put telepathy in so the town stalking turned worldwide with powers coming into it and send the individual on a made up "holiday" he would call it, where the individual would witness everyone knowing who it was and would seem like a weird, worldwide science-y experiment. He would introduce the word "messiah" and put it in telepathically, so the being thought it was a messenger in this weird scenario and that's why it was being stalked. Draconian would invent something called "money" needed to purchase things and create a financial situation so the being would have to keep going to work, or their job, he would call it and the next few years would descend into the being recognising faces, their own friends stalking themselves from university and from their own home town with a few characters thrown in. With his training, the being would learn to stop talking because it didn't want to be called crazy and God and calling the real universe heaven in religion, would be the being's ambition to be a suggested figure even if it didn't make sense to the being in the warp. He would make books, films and shows to train it, create a pretend home life and send it to his schools. He would place the real story into religion and set up Lucian as a demonic figure and the child, what he called an infant would learn the story of him leading one third of what he'd call immortals into killing God and failed and pretend Lucian was the ruler of Hell, his torture chamber, as punishment and leave out the massacre bit. He would call his fake world "Earth" and the robots humans. He would put in one religion: that evil humans went to Hell and good went to Heaven and with his training the individual would endure Draconian's made up job roles. He could get it done in 59 months, one month short of five years, with it being manageable with his training. He would put the being to what he called sleep from a baby at night time, to the end of it all, so the being could rest at night. With his training, the telepathy ongoing for all of it, and making the warp hazy and lessening the individual's focus, all factors would get the being through it all. He would try and put a magical robot friend in the cars, the vehicle he was going to use for gang-stalking and bond his being magically to it, maybe a baby to get them through; a baby that doesn't age as odd signs. It would take 23 years to train the child in the fake world at his schools and university.

A while later, Draconian had finished creating his fake world and planning all segments of training, the warp and his pretend end of Earth narrative and humans story, where he would pretend a programme went up and would put his face in a music video and pretend to move in, after bridging the individual away from fake Earth once it was over. This would mean the being had a boss and would be a supernatural miracle to the being and he or she would heal in his programme and be transitioned to the real universe and learn the truth about the whole thing. He or she would learn that Earth wasn't real and all were robots and he or she were pushed to transport the criminals, the story of Lucian and God being real, plus a massacre and resurrection and would learn about the hideaways. He would communicate through what he called the internet and emails and the being would understand why he or she couldn't join the real universe until he or she was healed from post-traumatic stress disorder and burnout. Draconian had decided to reward the individual for being made by him to be tormented, when the real universe was so amazing for all made, with a crown. He would reward the being with the title of ruler and he or she would rule with himself. Draconian decided to make the being female because he felt it would be easier to push a female over a male in a non-magical powers situation and would give the title queen and empress, the reward to rule with him. A position of power to say sorry and thank you. He would give the female magical powers once healed and transition her well to the real universe of open magic and prepare her for her reward, Queen training incorporated and magical powers. She would be happy in the future, finding out she will never die, believing humans age and die and will never age and can't be killed in the real universe either. She will find out that in the real universe there is the upgrade of TV, food, drink, games and books from Draconian selecting fivez of his inventions for training on a basic level in the fake world, so the selections were the right level for training. There was also much more that he had invented for her to feel excitement about. Draconian didn't want to torture anyone, but it was his only choice. The female would understand she wouldn't exist otherwise and had a great reward waiting and he would tell her via messages in the healing transition phase. It was the only way. Between the ages of 23–28, not knowing she hasn't aged, the female as trained, without knowing it would be pushed to transport. Tormented and tortured to transport. He was going to add in the 'jobs' and magical physical pain to cut it all down to just under five years. The female would be trained to handle the magic pain and wonder why she didn't die from it and worry sometimes.

Shortly later, his designed fake world was complete and would run automatically until the day healing and transitioning was over and he said hello in person and took the female into the real universe to be crowned Queen and Empress of his universe. Now, all there was left to do was finish making the female he had began sculpting. In 23–28 years he would have transported, sentenced and executed what he called the criminals and they'd be wiped out from existence, their own plan done back to themselves.

Chapter 16

Draconian had decided to make his champion the most beautiful being he had ever made. He wanted her to stand out. He didn't want to make her on the same beauty level as the others, because they may become bored with his champion and her queen reward if she wasn't astonishing to look upon, before the zillions left in his population, two thirds of the original total. He decided to make her skin a creamy white instead of the light brown used on himself and his universe, so her skin tone was different from all the rest. He came up with a new eye colour he had not used before, a light golden brown and made her hair black. As he finished making her mouth and nose he looked at his work and inhaled a short intake of breath. He could not believe his own work. He had made the most astonishingly beautiful woman he had ever made. He was in awe of his own creation. He felt bewilderment and awe that he had never felt before. He had never been lost for words at his own creation. His own work. He could not help staring in wonder. He had done the best work he had ever done. He could not believe how beautiful he had made her. He had made her smaller than the other women with hips, which made a beautiful hourglass figure. He loved the body he had made too with the white skin and the beautiful curvy form, from the rear end too. Draconian decided, as he stared in wonder, that he wanted her to belong to him. He wanted his beautiful creation to be his alone. How could he bind her to him forever? He started thinking about what new bond he could create between a man and a woman. More than friendship. He thought about her moving in with him, as opposed to making her her own home and living with him forever. How could he enjoy her and bond them together beyond friendship? Then he had an idea. An idea where he could enjoy her with the sight of no clothing on and make the most of his wonderful creation's body. He decided to add an organ onto his body and an entry path between the female's legs and create a form of pleasure for them to have with no clothing on. He would make the feeling of pleasure in the male's and female's body exhilarating, so they wanted to participate in the activity together, several times a day and all night. He began fashioning himself a body part between his legs and designing the female's too. When Draconian was done, he decided to name his new organ between his legs, a penis. When he was finished creating the female's body part between her legs, he named it a vagina. Draconian decided to enter the female to try out his invention. He entered and shivered with delight. He kept moving and moving and felt more and more delight at the wet response from the vagina he had designed and gloried in her face and body. He started to pant and make sounds at the unbelievable invention. As he carried on in ecstasy, he felt his creation, what he called an orgasm building up. It felt exhilarating. As he ejaculated in ecstasy, he collapsed on the female. It was the greatest thing he had ever invented. He decided to call it sex. Ejaculation was the word he made up for when his penis released a substance, when the experience was finishing the climax of sex. He wanted to try again, and turned the female around to have sex in another position so he could enjoy the sight of her from the back too. He magically made his penis erect again, the word he created for when he made his penis hard and entered her again and thought about putting her on top as well. He tried out every position he thought of and made up entering her rear-end too. He invented oral sex when thinking about putting his penis in her mouth and invented himself going down on her too and gave them both a different feeling of pleasure from the experience. The woman, during sex, would feel a rise in pleasure and ecstatically orgasm too. He brought the female only robotically to life at this point and enjoyed her riding on top of him too. He put his tongue in her mouth and massaged her tongue with his and called this kissing. He made her nipples a stimulating area and touched them as she rode him and she moaned in pleasure. He made up foreplay where they excited each other by touching stimulating areas before having sex. He would insert his finger into her vagina first and she could stroke him and move her hand up and down and he would ejaculate. When he was done and practically collapsing on the floor in amazement at his own invention, he wondered what to call this word. How he felt about the female and the desire he felt. He decided to call her his wife. And thought of a bonding ceremony to bind them together forever. He would call it a wedding and exchange rings and she would live with him forever. Draconian would introduce the concept of man and wife and sex and the organs on to his population, once he was ready to present his plan of transportation to his universe. He would conduct all his population's weddings, once they'd decided who they wanted to marry as he had decided to name it. Getting married. Marriage. Man and wife for eternity. Your soulmate forever. He decided on the word 'husband' for the man. The wedding term for the husband would be groom. The female the 'bride'. Everyone could have their own beautiful private ceremony with him, binding the couple together, and exchange rings and he would magic honeymoon destinations for each couple alone in a paradise, until they wanted to return and would merge every couple's palace and home together. As for him, he would have to wait for his bride, a baby, once made, to grow into an adult and turn 23 and be tortured to transport the criminals before she could know who he was. She would have to be healed and transitioned before he could marry her. He didn't know how he would cope with her beauty level and her not seeing him so decided that it would be best for him to downgrade her beauty in the fake world so he could cope with it when she grew into adulthood. He was going to set up their wedding from the fake world via the healing transitional stage. Draconian decided to name his wife. Draconian said, 'Rhea' to himself and found it beautiful and it suited his wife's face.

"I love you," Draconian said to his now still wife, the word he decided on to express his feelings.

He began designing Rhea at all ages from 0 to 23, her full grown age. He designed the baby and adored it. He robotically brought her to life and enjoyed the infant. She was jolly and happy and loveable and you couldn't help becoming besotted with the creation.

What a waste, he thought to himself, *that she'll never see me as a baby and I can only pop in in disguise to visit.*

Draconian pondered about loving his baby invention too, as a separate entity from his future love that it would turn into.

I know, Draconian thought. *I will have a male baby with Rhea and call it a son and a female and call it a daughter. They will grow inside her for nine months as she bonds with them both and when they come out easily we'll raise them together. I'll call myself their father or dad, and Rhea will be their mother or mum. They'll be our children and I'll offer the possibility of two to every couple and they can raise them together. Our children can have children and we'll call them our grandchildren and great grandchildren after that. I'll call this a family. My own will be the royal family, and I'll call my son the prince, my daughter the princess and so their children shall be too! This is perfect and I'll incorporate it all into Rhea's training.* Draconian made some amendments to Rhea's training and changed her home life to having a robot mother and father and siblings is what he named the relationship between the son and daughter. Brother and sister. He would write the parents and sister robots out of Rhea's existence as he did with all and put in other relative robots too, called uncles, aunts and cousins as he thought up words for all future relationships between families. The universe would be happy and exciting in the future as everyone's children married one another too. He thought about his invention sex and would put magic down so it was not possible for anyone to take part in sexual activity with anyone but their husband and wife and his Universe would remain wonderful instead of any problems arising from his inventions. He would disguise himself as what he named a boyfriend to Rhea, in her what he named teenage years from 13–19. He would come in disguise as three boyfriends. One, a friend at 13 where he would only kiss her and arrange a pretend break up. He would magic in her feeling attraction to the boys and then get rid of it. He would then be a best friend turned boyfriend for only two weeks and magic away the attraction. At 16, he would ask her to be his girlfriend again in another disguise and would have sex with her at 17. He wouldn't let her experience full orgasm sex in the fake world as she may not be able to live without it and would be too much of a big deal with his disguise, so he would downgrade it and make it shorter, only a few minutes long and put enough pleasure in, for her to enjoy it and be able to stop for when he arranged the break up at 19, after her first year at his University in the fake world. He'd place himself in a music video and would telepathically come into it and let her see the odd image of him, not clearly in the fake world, really vaguely. He would swap roles with Lucian and pretend he was the non-evil version who was misunderstood and pretend God was bad and destroyed on the made up date of 4th July 2018 when it would be over for Rhea, the criminals transported. This way she could become attracted to his form on TV the downgraded version and would want to marry him knowing it was an ideal situation. He'd pretend giving birth was painful, so suggesting children and living forever, never aging and no such thing as death after the failed massacre would be a win win situation. She would be bonded and love him as a downgraded being, an immortal, not as the Creator and tell her two years into the learning bridge. This would mean when he put his neck shift in for the move in part, where she finds she has a boss now who can't reveal himself because she needs to be healed and transitioned to the real universe and moved on from the fake, she would feel attraction and awkwardness at that point due to her PTSD (post-traumatic stress disorder). When he told her he was the creator and it was all the other way around instead of pretending God was jealous of him when he made himself and taught her the truth of it all, she would love him for his face on the videos, a as opposed to who and what he really was and when she found out it wouldn't make a difference. He would romance her by putting in flowers and messages and telling her he was in love with her and telling her his story. She would be his wife, as well as Queen as her reward and mother and grand-mother as he called it to his children and grandchildren. He would love her forever. The explanation in the fake world for her existence would be being born from sex between her mother and father and he would set up his own union with herself through his fake world and disguises.

When Draconian had amended the programme to fit in his future plans, he stepped into it. He was in what he called a hospital with the mother robot called Meena. He had the still baby form of Rhea in his arms. He kissed her on the forehead and placed her in the robot's arms He turned invisible and magicked Rhea to life. She opened her eyes and stared gurgling up at her robot mother and so Rhea's strange, fake world transporter destiny began. Draconian looked at the baby adoringly one more time and left, leaving his magical transportation programme to run on auto.

Chapter 17

Draconian's universe celebrated the transportation plan when he told them of it and showed them all and showed all the villains being transported. They celebrated the reward for Rhea upon watching how the criminals, their enemies would be transported. When he announced that he had fallen in love, a new word for all, they were intrigued. When he introduced sex and marriage to them, they all celebrated and had a wonderful time deciding which closest male or female friend they should marry. When it came to their wedding nights and experiencing sex for the first time, they all celebrated Draconian's invention and loved the idea of doing it for eternity with their partner. They thought it was the greatest invention ever and awaited the arrival of Rhea his own wife and future Queen, after the transporting was finished and they all lived happily in peace.

Draconian loved the baby Rhea and looked forward to his own babies with her. He had made up DNA and put it in everyone so the babies would be formed from the appearances of both parents DNA mixing, as he called it, the role of mother and father. He popped into the fake world Earth every day to talk to child Rhea in disguise and watched her blossom into a 13 year old, attending his schools every day in the uniform he invented, thinking the formula of existence was school, university job, age and death, get married and have children. He had made it so the robots would all look the same as 12 at 23, so it de-threatened the gang-stalking at 23. The majority would be short. He would make the speech stupid in Rhea's fake world home town and robots stupid, so Rhea mentally corrected the majority's English and pretended Rhea was a minority in the country she lived in and hadn't picked up her native language, to make marriage unappealing and taught the female's role was to cook for her husband and family and made it so Rhea didn't know how to cook and could only look after herself, when she moved into his accommodation for university 45 minutes away, on his made up underground train line. He'd designed it so the news it was never the real world one day, would be great for Rhea and she'd wake up happy at the truth every morning, once it was over and happy for her future prospects in the real universe.

When Rhea turned 13, he popped in as her first boyfriend and named himself Larim. He asked her out after kissing her on the cheek, at his made up spin the bottle game, at a house party she attended. Rhea never knew that was the only time a real being was in her world, the rest of the time she was being trained by his robots. He brought Rhea a chain saying Princess to tell her of the future but had conjured it in really without her knowing. He went to the downgraded cinema with her and kissed her for nearly two years. He remembered the first time they kissed properly instead of just on the cheek or a peck after she turned 14. March 2004 the made up year. In the real universe they were several million years in. He had made up the history of Earth, so Rhea thought it was billions of years old but they called it the 90s and noughties by her time and the year 2000.

Draconian felt sad when it was time for his disguise as Larim to come to an end, before it got to his disguise's and Rhea's two year anniversary. With magic she forgot about it in two weeks and had a new group of friends, the robot friends around her called 'the crew' as he'd designed for her training. He was also training her to be Queen without her knowing and his wife and mother and grandmother to his children and grand-children. He'd incorporated his disguises into her training, Rhea with no idea that her life and existence would change into a warp at 23 and a half. His robot organized a 16th birthday party for Rhea which she loved and was important for her training. He made sure that she loved her life up to 23 years, even though he added in arguing to Rhea's home life and one domestic issue where the father beat the mother in front of her when she was ten, with her robot sisters watching. This was to train her for the summer of 2013 when his warp began. Along with his invention of horror films and books, she read and along with all her lessons in his schools to mentally train her for what he called gang-stalking and the warp with telepathy. Two months after Rhea's 16 birthday party, he asked her out again, in the disguise of one of her good friends called Romano. It only lasted two weeks because as arranged she found it too weird going out with her good friend, but he got to kiss her again and enjoyed the two weeks in the disguise as one of his robots. In the summer of the made up year of 2006, Rhea took what she thought was her big exams called GCSEs for training. In September 2006, when she started what was called sixth form and began wearing suits in her training, he asked her out again. This time his disguise was as a malem from another school in the fake town of robots, his made up name Idab. He pretended via the robots that he beat up boys in the area so everyone was scared of him and made up the story line of the rest of the robots in town acting scared of him, so Rhea didn't want a boyfriend after this one was over. He made it the long one with three year two months and made up that Rhea had to marry the same religion as herself, so couldn't marry his disguise. He waited six months as Rhea thought she'd made up and finally took her clothes off and entered her. He'd loved removing her clothing for the three months up to that point and inserting his finger into her as she moved his penis up and down causing him to ejaculate. He called the first time the taking of her virginity. He met up with her in disguise every other day and had sex every other day. He had sex in park bushes and pretend hotel rooms. Rhea invited him around to her house later in the relationship, thinking it was a secret from her parents, whom she was afraid of as she wasn't allowed to have boyfriends in the fake world. This was when she thought they'd gone out. He made love to her in his own shelter for her and loved every intimate moment they shared.

When Rhea was 18, she finished her time at what he called secondary school, after primary school until 11. She did her made up big exams he named A Levels. She went to what she thought was a top university in the country she lived in called England. In her accommodation he made love to her and she orgasmed for the first time when he performed oral sex on her. She loved sex from the amount of pleasure he put in and felt ecstasy, the right amount for the fake world, as she experienced it. In December 2008 in his disguise, he asked if Rhea wanted to break up due to having no future. She said yes as planned and he carried on seeing her for another eight months, slowly easing her out of the relationship. When Rhea, in his plan stopped meeting up with himself due to him magicking out the attraction and magicking in what he called a crush, Rhea moved on from his disguise. He sorely missed her and being intimate with her but could cope from downgrading her beauty. He was still in love with the face he had created even when downgraded but could handle not being seen with the downgraded beauty level as he had his transportation war to conduct. Criminals to capture.

He watched his programme and popped in in disguise only as a friend to talk to Rhea, after that point. He watched her enjoy the night life of clubs with friends he had put in for training and her life changed to loving going out and dancing to music. He watched her on his social media website he had created, where you could become friends with friends and acquaintances on it and write on each other's pages. This is how he would also set up his gang-stalking from her recognising people from it driving past her in person and lip reading about them hacking into her accounts. She was being highly trained for the entire warp. Once university had finished he gave Rhea the made up job of teaching assistant, working in his schools so she could enjoy his made up holidays after each term was finished. This was the most enjoyable training he could come up with. He saved his call centre invention with no robot naughty children for during the warp, so he could push her with angry voice recordings she would think were people calling her in the warp. He set up pretend money problems at home pretending Rhea's robot father's second business was failing and she gave money from her scholarship money to help in his narrative which changed her in her training. It would mean she would have to stay in her next teaching assistant job for money as his story line was her father moving to another country and pretending to start a business and leaving them in debt. The time of the warp drew nearer and nearer. 22. 23. 7 months after Rhea's 23rd birthday it was time. She had started the made up job of secondary school teaching assistant and was about to start her summer holiday and go abroad on holiday too with her pretend flat mates from university. The background had always shifted when travelling, unbeknown to Rhea.

24th July 2013, the made up year finally came around and Rhea's existence turned to a summer of terror.

Chapter 18

It began with her going to her friend's house and thinking she saw one of the male's there say he was taking pictures of her to send to a friend. On auto, she started losing focus on TV from there. Draconian activated her powers around about this time. On the following Thursday the beginning of August she saw four boys drive past that she recognized from social media and seen in person from a distance a few times and lip read them say that one male, her friend had name dropped, who went to prison for selling cocaine, Draconian's made up stories, had hacked into her bank account. Rhea suddenly became terrified and very nervous. She went to stay with her old flat mate that weekend and upon return saw a male parked outside her house. She looked through the window and saw him there later in the evening too. She informed her mother and family and her mother said later in the week that she was a schizophrenic. A made up word for a mental disorder. Rhea carried on acting normal and saw the one she thought had gone to prison that Draconian had named , Riz, drive past with one of the male robots from the car. She even cancelled her cards and went to the bank to ask about hacking. On the Sunday, after Rhea went out to a party on Saturday night a pretend engagement party, feeling furious at being hacked, as planned, Rhea received telepathy which told her she wasn't having a nervous breakdown as her mother had suggested. When she went abroad it got wider and she thought she was in a weird science experiment. On the way back from holiday the telepathy made her think she had landed the plane by itself. This was to make her think she was something more than human. On her return she heard the word messiah and her path of thinking it all had something to do with God began. In September she returned to the secondary school Cranfields. This time she was in a warp with telepathy on and pretending nothing was going on. The weird summer and religious suggestions turned into stalking. She saw the males from social media and the drive by, drive past every single day and saw her own friends from University and her home town drive by at all times as well. She carried on with her social life pretending and saw their faces when she went for a drive with her friends. She felt betrayed as she knew her siblings and mother and father and everyone was in on it, no one saying a word. She learned to stay silent because she didn't want to get called crazy. Weird stories came in through her telepathy like the drivers having sex with animals and participating in weird sex practices. Draconian put this in to de-threaten them. This meant that Rhea wasn't afraid to walk around by herself during it or in the evenings. Rhea wrote in diaries as suggested by her robot mother, to write down what was occurring. In November she thought a baby from a picture in social media was her soulmate when he drove past and became her telepathic friend, she saw drive past everyday too and stole attention away from the stalkers. Draconian put this in to get Rhea through the torment and later in added a baby brother too and made both beautiful for the robot level.

Rhea didn't pass her probation at work and cried and moved house and city with her robot mother leaving the hometown. Draconian did this to roll her out of the fake and move her on from her hometown. She moved to the north and he put her in a call centre role for three months and then moved her back to the made up city of London. He eventually rolled her out of socializing with all friends in the last year of it. Rhea continued on in the warp, feeling betrayed, writing in her diaries, hating being stalked. She wrote a book and poetry that was magicked in by Draconian really to get her by. She experienced the physical pain as well and was scared of dying, thinking she was being poisoned by the human race. A beacon of hope came with Draconian's made up terrorist attacks on the human population. Rhea celebrated their deaths. He put in her head that one of the male stalkers was being treated like a prophet instead of her, even though she didn't know what she was and put in a suggestion she couldn't die and she wondered if they were trying to kill her invisibly, as he'd put in her head that they turned invisible in front of her and wondered if they stabbed her invisibly and she never died, which was why she was being stalked. The years rolled on and Rhea suffered and moved from call centre job to call centre job. She acted and never said a word about the stalking out loud. The story line was her being a messenger of God, even if she didn't know how, because in one of the religions there had been a man who performed miracles of magic. She didn't know what she was or why she was in this warp and why the human race as a whole, no matter where she went joined in on her stalking and the home town faces were everywhere, everyday; her only power the strange telepathy which wasn't reading the minds of all those around her. She was furious at it all and there was nothing to do but endure a line in a film she'd seen before it happened. The years went on until Rhea was almost at five years. After her third call centre role, fourth job role during the warp, with some administration, she didn't know if she had it in her to do a fifth warp call centre job as they had made her last role too demanding and pushed her out of it. She didn't know what the point of all this was but had received symbols on her hands in the December that had just passed. The symbols just formed letters and pictures and in February 2018 a boy band member from a band called K-s-y had come into it. It was the same face, maybe the best looking on TV from the 90s and his name was JK. He had arrived in it magically somehow and she could see him vaguely in some weird third eye way described in a fantasy book she had read before the warp. He acted like he was in love with her and references to him entered it all. She wanted to go to heaven and didn't mind being God's champion for whatever reason if that was the case. She didn't know how she would have made it through without her soulmate connection to the baby in the car that she called Kiki and his baby brother Zax. She wondered why both never aged from the car window or in social media pictures. They had taken the attention away from the stalkers so couldn't imagine it without them.

Chapter 19

From the moment the warp started, Draconian started capturing his first killers. He had made cells for them to be transported into, where their powers would be stripped. He brought them out televised for his world to see. Each town and planet going to watch the execution in person of their own killers and traitor friends for many. When the first hundred arrived, he brought them out continuously in lines of ten, so he could speak to each one face to face.

"You scum," he told them all. They stood there looking scared. Some begged.

"Please, Draconian, Lucian made us. It was Rozzio, Serline and Feraz with Lucian. They made us."

"I know everything," said Draconian. "About your envy. And for the crime of the mass murder of the entire Universe and trying to transport me into a torture chamber for eternity, you will have your own weapon used against you. You will be the ones who no longer exist," and he sent Lucian's own creation the weapon used by them all, the lethal killing magic, flying towards them all. They screamed and were wiped from existence. He did this again and again everyday of Rhea's torment, the criminals all being transported in. When the vortex arrived in the hide away containing the one third and they all saw a number of them get transported away, there was great panic and the third all tried to flee into another hide away. But it kept coming every time they fled, the big black tornado, consuming them, coming everyday and getting more and more of them.

When Serline, Feraz and Rozzio arrived in their cells , Draconian stood the three before him for his universe to see on television and the friends they'd betrayed there with him.

"You three. After all I gave you. You tried to transport me into a torture chamber for eternity and helped organize the destruction of the entire universe. Do you have anything to say for yourselves, scum? "Draconian asked.

"We're sorry," said Serline. "We were just so jealous."

"You only doomed yourselves you who had everything. I gave you everything. You're the fools who got bribed with glory from Lucian and failed," said Draconian.

"And the penalty is your own weapon used against you. Goodbye and good riddance," said Draconian and wiped them all from existence with their own weapon.

Chapter 20

Lucian was sitting in his garden as he had been doing for 23 years. Lounging and sipping on a drink and listening to music. All of a sudden, he felt himself flying.

"Arghhhhhhhhhh," he screamed. Astounded, with no idea about what going on. He fell into a white padded room moments later. He looked around him. He tried to use his magic to get out. He stared at his hands, no magic coming out of them. *Fly,* he thought to himself.

"Arghhhhhhhhh," he screamed again. Realizing he'd been caught. *How?* he thought fearfully as he knew he was going to come face to face with his maker.

When Draconian teleported him in front of himself, Lucian stood and stared.

"Lucian," said Draconian. "The traitor and scum. Organiser of the massacre of the universe. Inventor of your dark magic and designer of my torture chamber. All which you failed with. I resurrected all moments later and all carried on living. Here, the friends you betrayed and massacred stood before you too."

"Do you have anything to say for yourself?" Draconian asked.

"How did you transport me to yourself?" asked Lucian. "Is all I have to say."

Draconian showed him how he did it, showing him the reel of Rhea as he'd shown the rest. "I'm transporting them all. Connecting powers to emotions that's how I get the speed to beat your alarm and transport you all," said Draconian.

"Ah," said Lucian, "Clever as always. I never thought it would be possible to catch us."

"Scum!" roared his friends.

"Traitors," said others.

"There's nothing left to do or say but sentence you as I've done with the rest. You're going to be eradicated and erased from existence the way you planned and organized for everyone else. You'll be wiped out by your own invention. Your downfall. Me getting the idea of how to get the speed from your torture chamber," said Draconian.

"Noooooooooooooooooooooooo," screamed Lucian.

"Don't, please. I'm sorry," said Lucian, falling to his knees.

"You've said your last words, Lucian," said Draconian. He conjured Lucian's lethal weapon into his hand, a blazing orange and flung it towards himself. Lucian a lit with the orange glow was incinerated, screaming. Until there was nothing left of him but the empty spot, he'd been kneeling in.

The room was silent. He was gone.

After 23 years of hiding.

Chapter 21

As the years went on, the three organizers caught at the beginning of the warp, along with Lucian the creator of it all, due to there only being three in their hide away and only Lucian in his, Draconian watched Rhea and executed the masses being transported in daily, after their demise. He felt terrible watching Rhea but it was the only way and she could survive it all, not knowing it would be over one day. It's only a matter of days he had put in her head at the beginning. He watched her light golden brown eyes glaze over after the third year, the sparkle once there being lost. He'd heal and transition her and she'd celebrate the truth one day and would wake up happy every morning about the truth of her existence and money and jobs not being real. Until she learned that they had always been robots, which was the only logical explanation for it all and would be excited for the prospect of all he told her he had invented in the real universe and living forever with magical powers and getting married to him and having full sex one day and babies with him. He watched her endure and do every day he had planned out. He had put the word sabbatical in for after her call centre role after moving back to London, so she had a break. The fourth role was the last long slog. He had written out her friend robots and she would be happy when her pretend family were erased too.

Finally after almost five years nearly all had been transported. The end narrative began for Rhea. A miracle happened and she received a revelation, as suddenly when she typed she was receiving messages. She got her first made up human explanation for it about being a messenger, even though it made no sense. She was over the moon. The next day she received what she thought was contact from entities she couldn't see, who had come across her plight and had gone out and started destroying Earth's population. The population went down to thousands to hundreds. And on 2nd July 2018 the made up year, it went down to 10. Rhea celebrated. Only her robot mother and sisters were alive. In the next few days, he wrote out the few remaining as planned, pretending some were making it into heaven with her and for telepathic friends, without her thinking about not seeing them and even brought himself in as a mini me too to guide her, who she could hear and see in the weird third eye way as she thought of it. She'd seen a glitch in the air around her when she whacked an insect with a broom and saw that a programme went up over Earth. He made her siblings and mother horrible for the few weeks as Rhea felt burned out and put a made up story in her head about an immortal war and gods she couldn't see. He eventually pretended the three, mother and sisters had been killed without her seeing, and she relaxed living in the programme grateful for resources and thought the mini me was her child with Draconian's, who had lived with her invisibly for years never aging and the two baby soulmates were out there with her father and one cousin's cute child. Eventually the miracle of JK moving in happened when she saw his neck shift and she experienced her first big supernatural occurrence and retired from the mental pressure of what was going on as she'd been trained to carry on and had a boss. In the next few months, with the setting up of watching TV shows and resting and and some walks, Draconian eventually erased earth from existence through his messages running on auto and erased the characters she thought were her telepathic friends still. He told her the baby soulmates was his magic to get her through and in this time told her it was his side's plan with him pretending God was bad and himself Lucian's character, the misunderstood version, and told her all were robots. It was the only logical solution for it all, to be an immortal war because the human and earth explanation made no sense. He successfully erased the human race with made up sex stories by making it telepathically silly. The next year he flipped it around and told her he was the Creator and he made the real universe outside. He bridged her well with his stories, learning parts of it here and there and bringing it all together at the right time in line with her healing. He put in flowers and told her of his plans for the future of marrying him and told her through his messages that he was her boyfriends in disguise, and she'd had sex with him and sex was his invention and she'd only kissed him. This helped him create a bond with her as she continued to watch his music videos where he upgraded his appearance slightly.

Outside, on the 4th July 2018 in the fake world, Draconian's Universe celebrated as he sentenced and executed the last of the criminals. It was over. Over for Rhea. And over for themselves. His Universe was at peace. The traitors dead. No more hideaways. The universe was one again. His world rejoiced and celebrated. And celebrated himself and his trained champion, the transporter.

It took years to heal and bridge Rhea to the real universe. He popped in in disguise to see her every day. For the first one and a half years he told her he was every being she saw on the road and then loosened her to all being robots and himself just popping in. She knew everything around three to three and a half years in. She knew she'd been made and trained by him in a fake world of robots to be tortured and pushed to transport the criminals, the killers and Lucian and the three, in the three hideaways, so her creator could transport them to himself and sentence and execute them so his world was at peace again. He erased what wasn't real and taught her what was. He was glad she knew who he was and arranged for her to order a poster for himself to put on her wall. He changed her shelter around two and a half years in. He prepared her for magical powers as she healed from PTSD and burnout and put in some magical bits and bobs along the way to prepare her. He introduced schemes to help her along in it to help her with magic whilst she rested.

Finally years later the day finally arrived for Draconian to show himself to her and start his love life.

Chapter 22

Draconian opened the door to the living room in the shelter he'd created for Rhea.

"Hello," he said in his own form.

Rhea gasped as he said she would, shocked at his beauty and real form.

"Hello," Rhea said.

"As you know I made you and I've taught you everything about why you were made and what my warp was for and my training and you know we're at peace now and you were my transporter made and trained, without knowing it and pushed. You know I'm the creator of my universe and all in it, all who are dead now and of course yourself and the fake world you thought was Earth. You know that I'm rewarding you with a crown and I want you to rule my universe with me and be Queen and Empress, the title I made up for it. You know I love you and I fell in love making you and invented marriage and want to have two babies and a family with you, with grandchildren and great grandchildren. So, you know the day was going to come where I'd ask and I'm getting to it straight away. Will you, Rhea, my love, marry me?" asked Draconian.

"I will," said Rhea. Knowing for years that Draconian was going to ask her to marry him via his messages.

"I think it's time I told you my real name, instead of calling me Creator forever," said Draconian. "It's Draconian."

"Draconian," Rhea repeated.

"I'm so sorry for the terrible torture, Rhea. You'll love being Queen and you're going to love having magical powers, living in my palace and luxury for eternity. Everyone is lovely and friendly in the real universe and you'll love it all and you'll love me and your children forever," Draconian told Rhea.

Rhea could not believe how beautiful he was and that she was going to be making love to this being for eternity and was going to fall in love as he'd told her and couldn't believe he was her three boyfriends in disguise, in the past. Idab an anagram for a boyfriend in disguise. She found Draconian's face ideal in the videos but this was on a whole different level. She was still bewildered by his face, by the time it came to exiting the fake world.

They sat and talked on the sofas for a while and then Draconian put his hands on her shoulders and said, "I'm giving you your powers."

His hands glowed for a moment, and she felt a joyous rush. He took his hands off her shoulders.

"You will never age. You will live forever. You will have magical powers. You will be Queen. You will love being married to me and you will love having a family one day, after billions of years of enjoying married life with me and you'll love your reward and your powers and all my inventions," Draconian told her.

He opened a portal in the air. He held out his hand.

"Come. Let me take you out of here forever. Let me show you how to fly," said Draconian.

Rhea put her hand in Draconian's hand feeling a rush of excitement and awe, still bewildered by his beauty.

"Take one last look at the fake world," said Draconian.

Rhea looked back with him one more time and stepped out of her fake existence into the real universe.

***

After Rhea had got to know Draconian, in a place he had made for just the two of them, she had fallen in love, as he said she would and married him in a beautiful private ceremony and said her vows to him whilst exchanging rings. She promised to love him forever and be married to him for eternity, as he did with her and then they exchanged rings.

That night, with excitement Draconian finally got to make love to his wife Rhea, after waiting for what felt like forever and was happy for the rest of eternity living with his wife and making love to her every day and night.

Rhea ruled by his side happily as Queen, loved her husband and her creator, and billions of years later loved the children and family she had with him.

Draconian's universe of Alaskia was at peace and happy forever and Draconian and Rhea were in love and happy for the rest of eternity.

THE END